# THE WANDERING SHEEP

# THE WANDERING SHEEP

## Courage to Pursue
## the Path Within

*Part 1*

## WARREN O'BRYAN-ADAMS

EMPOWERED VISIONS PRESS

Empowered Visions Press
A division of Unlimited Empowered Visions LLc
Atlanta, Ga 30344

Library of Congress Control Number: 2020922695

ISBN: (Print): 978-1-7327947-0-2
ISBN (Ebook): 978-1-7327947-1-9

Cover design by Euan Monaghan
Edited by Pam Elise Harris

www.whoiswarrenobryan.com

*To the couch surfing artist,*
*Surf on until you catch your wave.*

*The crownless again shall be king.*

**J.R.R. TOLKIEN**

# CONTENTS

## PREFACE

The teacher went down each row: Tell me, what do you want to be in the future?

Even in elementary school, there was a desperate need to know about the future. Someplace where all humans eventually end up once you complete your education and graduate from college.

"How am I supposed to know about the future when it hasn't come yet?" I thought to myself. The future seemed so far away.

One by one, each of my classmates roared

out loud with dreams: of becoming doctors, lawyers, professional singers, firefighters, and police officers. It filled the room. None of those jobs fit the idea of what I saw myself doing. After a while, I became bored hearing everyone repeat the same answers, so I wandered off, looking out the window, staring at the leaves falling from the trees.

"Warren O'Bryan, it is your turn. Stand up. What do you want to be in the future?" the teacher asked.

I slowly began to rise out of the seat, trying to come up with an answer before standing tall.

I stood there, twiddling my fingers nervously as silence filled the room. I said nothing while all of my classmates waited for my answer. The only thing I could think to do was close my eyes, hoping that some answer would come.

The fiery words "I want to help people be free!" came flying from my lips.

I was surprised by my answer, mostly

embarrassed. My classmates began to laugh. One kid even shouted out, "That's stupid!"

"Okay, how do you want to help people be free?" the teacher asked with a puzzled look on her face.

"I don't know yet," I replied.

American writer Henry David Thoreau famously said, "The mass of men lead lives of quiet desperation."

I didn't know of Thoreau in my younger years, but I've always known I was not going to live a life of quiet desperation, lament, and defeat. I would face up to life, all its happiness and hurdles, all its opportunities and anguish. I was going to see it, identify it, explore it, and ask questions of it. And, yes, I was going to write about it. Even if, at times—indeed most times—it would come with some pain and doubt; but no journey worth taking is bliss.

**As a student, I looked out into the world**

**with wonder; you can say I was intellectu-
ally curious about life.**

- How did we arrive here?
- How did society become as it is?
- Why were people who looked like me
  tucked away in the shadows of American history?

I wanted to *know* why things were the way
they were, but answers weren't often found
where my young mind searched.

*"Warren O'Bryan, you ask too many questions;
things are the way they are."* It is what so many
teachers often told me. I promised myself each
time I encountered this answer that I would
not kneel before "the way things are." As an
eager learner, the way things are never sat well
with me.

Anyone who has a heritage that once included
shackles and chains in their lineage knows the

scars that silence can leave. At its core, that is why an answer of silence to a question asked could never resonate with me. Silence is a threat to all who prize justice. If my people's history taught me anything, it's that accepting the way things are was a surefire guarantee we would always kneel. Change only happens via the bravery of those who dare with bold audacity to say, "The way things are will never be the way things should be."

Early on in the public education system, I grew exhausted from American history that rarely showed people who looked like me. People who stepped forward and spoke, wrote, sang, and marched. Human beings who said: as long as the chains are locked, the road to real freedom for all Americans is closed. People who saw the way things were and showed us how they could be.

I grew weary of the rules and standardized tests that tried to streamline lies. I rebelled against it. For every lesson taught, I asked in-depth questions. It seemed the more questions I asked, the more trouble I got myself into. So much trouble that my voice eventually turned inward, and I internalized my inquiries about the world.

But while my lips were shut, my soul never stopped stirring, daring me to write what I knew to be true.

I was in $7^{th}$ grade and got wind that we would be getting a school newspaper; here was my chance to question things out loud. I was offered the job to write my very own column. However, I didn't make it past two posts before being let go. Teachers, faculty, and staff deemed my posts too radical and controversial. I was hurt, devastated, and again compartmentalized my real thoughts of how I felt from that moment on. Rather than viewing my dismissal as a dishonor, I saw it as confirmation: I must keep on. I must question. I must be curious and continue writing even if no one reads it.

And most importantly, I must not apologize for being true to myself. I would apologize if I were not. I would say sorry to myself, to my people's history, and to the promise of what could have been reached in the future.

I was recently asked why I continue to write when I haven't made a dime from it in all these years?

Every writer finds in themselves a reason to write. I write for the dreamers, the artists, and soul searchers of truth. I write for the young kid inside of us all longing to be heard as an adult. I write for the silent thinkers who may never find the courage to think out loud because courage is not an option in their world now. It is essential. It is the defense against danger; it is the promise of a new path forward.

I believe every soul is here to help humanity progress and evolve in some way. The trick is pushing past a particular kind of programming of the mind that is no fault of your own.

My goal herein seeks to discover a creative way to add to the expansion of the human potential, and the journey thus far has led me here as a writer at this moment in time, and I must fulfill that calling.

**1**

## THE BLACK SHEEP

*You should ask yourself who*
*taught you to hate yourself.*

**MALCOLM X**

"I am ugly!" Emmanuel grappled with the rage, thick as mucus, that crawled up his throat. The words slithered across his tongue like the deadliest venom and curled outwardly through his lips, hitting its target. "God, why you did have to make me so damn ugly." This self-declaration, which had been suppressed and denied the freedom of expression, finally rose up to take its rightful place. It was true; he was, in fact, ugly. His skin was covered by flaky, cracked, and burned patches that caused him to look purple from the many years of applying fade creams. He disliked the texture of his chemically induced hair that hid his tight, knotted curls. He hated the scars left on both sides of his round nose from the laundry pins clipped there to thin it out. Since birth, Emmanuel was always in some sort of transformation at the hands of his mother. He had grown to despise himself just as she did for having been born with such ethnic features and dark skin. His eyes flared with anger as both of his hands firmly gripped the mirror. He stared at his fourteen-year-old self in search of any part that he admired, any part that would make him crawl back into bed and stay there. Nothing.

He stood up from the desk and curled his arms over his head, legs planted wide. The final verdict stared back at him in the mirror. It was clear he didn't belong in this family, and the house where he lay his head down every evening was not his home. There were

no happy memories of his birthday celebra-
tion, no jolly Christmas festivities, the Tooth
Fairy never left any money under his pillow,
nor were there any bedtime stories told. All
these realizations made themselves visible like
lightning during a rainstorm.

He turned away from the mirror and
pointed the flashlight around the orderly bedroom, decorated like an ad out of a home decor
magazine. Picture perfect. Everything he
needed for a successful future was provided: a
shelter, a bed for rest, food to eat, and clothes
to wear; and yet, with all of this, still he spent
most of his time daydreaming of one day
disappearing into the peaceful blue-painted
walls of the bedroom that camouflaged the
hell he truly lived in. He had learned how to
dwell in alternate realities that cast out the
dark clouds that lingered over his head. He'd
trained himself to carefully tiptoe through the
house unnoticed, only making his presence
known by undone chores. Any opportunity
for a new identity or purpose, he would have

gladly taken, just to feel—to know—what it meant to be loved.

Emmanuel grabbed the raggedy notebook marked with the letter 'C' from the desk and tucked it inside of his pants. He tiptoed to the closet and pulled apart the doors, mindful not to disturb anyone asleep. He flashed the light on his pressed Catholic school uniforms, hung neatly in front. If he could rip them apart or destroy them in any way, he would have. Catholic school, although religious in its intent, was no safe haven for him. He faced almost the same discrimination there as he did at home, being one of the only students of color. In fact, he was the darkest one to walk the halls of the prestigious school. He gently moved the uniforms to the side until he came to an old jacket tucked in the back of the closet. He reached inside and grabbed the hidden peculiar object, pressed it against his lips, then tucked it inside his pants pocket.

He slid his shoes on and paced back and forth nervously from the window to the bedroom door. His eyes gazed up above his bed at the empty space on the wall from where his awards once hung. It went unnoticed that they had been taken down and gone missing, even by his OCD mother. No one paid attention to his achievements, just his failures. So what else would a teenager do but search for love in the most rebellious way?

A shadow appeared in the window, followed by three taps. A surge of excitement rushed through Emmanuel's body. For once, he had found a group of friends that he could be himself around, where he could speak what he felt without every word being screened for its proper pronunciation. These friends embraced him, watched out for him, and adored him more than his own family, or so at least he thought.

## 2

## VOODOO CHILD

*The revolution has always been in the hands of the young. The young always inherit the revolution.*

**HUEY NEWTON**

It was the darkest part of the morning, when old homes creaked, popped, and made all sorts of strange noises. The kinds of sounds that creep deep within walls, scratch at ceilings, and thump on wooden stairs, but those who hear them pretend not to. That is what eight-year-old Jean-Jacques (no last name) did on the morning of August 28, 2005, as he awoke from a terrifying nightmare in Crescent City, Louisiana. His eyes opened just as the bedroom door closed shut. Alarmed by the unusual occurrence, his eyes gazed at the alarm clock on his nightstand: 3:00 a.m. Ever since that summer night on St. John's Eve at Lake Pontchartrain, he had awakened at that exact time. Like always, the hazy memory of that night made itself visible in his mind.

On the eve of June 25, every home was marked with a red strip of paint, placed at the top of their front doors. It was put there to ward off the wickedness that wandered the city on their special night. Any native of Crescent City carried on with the tradition whether they believed it to be true or not. Jean-Jacques, like everyone else in town, heard the strange tales about "The Voodoos" and all of their satanic rituals, lustful orgies, and, the most hideous of them all, the sacrificing of innocent children. If any of it was true, he was about to find out. On the ghostly night of St. John's Eve while the reddish tinge of moon glowed down on the city and ashen fog wavered through the streets, Jean-Jacques found himself hidden in the trunk of his Granme's parked car. He climbed his way out, greeted by the sounds of chirping crickets, croaking frogs, and murky rolling water. Fearless of the many exotic creatures that roamed in swamplands, his curiosity outweighed any fear. He continued on his quest, following the mysterious voices that echoed in the distance. When he edged as close as he could behind the armor of a bald cypress tree, he paused to examine the hidden campfire.

As he leaned closer, head tilted to the side, he witnessed a circle of individuals all holding hands and dressed in long, elegant black robes.

Like a sorcerer appearing out of thin air, his Granme emerged in the middle of the circle, with her arms stretched outward toward the blazing fire. Then, one by one, they all stripped naked and began clapping and chanting in a barbaric language. Their feet stomped at the ground, and the trees started to shake, and the louder they roared, the higher the campfire rose. Then, remarkably, the fire spiraled up from the ground into the air, forming a hollow vortex. The ground shook underneath Jean-Jacques's feet as he tensely clutched the tree. His amazement quickly transformed into fear. Out from the flaming ring of the vortex appeared a group of otherworldly monsters, black as night with long horns protruding from their foreheads. Jean-Jacques covered his mouth, his eyes glazed with disbelief. He nervously moved his feet backward, careful not to make his presence known. After turning around, withdrawn, a white puff of smoke was blown into his eyes, knocking him unconscious. He woke the next morning, sure he dreamed it all.

Unnerved by the memory, Jean-Jacques rolled onto his back and pulled the covers up over his head. His small fidgety hands nervously searched for the flashlight that he slept with every night. It could not be found. Like a boulder hitting a brick wall, his chest caved in and knocked the breath from his body. Paralyzed with fear, his jaws clenched shut as a warm sensation crawled down his legs, cementing his body to the piddle-soaked sheets. He had no other choice but to call out to his brother, Emmanuel.

"Manny, he whispered. Manny, wake up, I had the dream again." There was no reply. A fluttering feeling rose in his stomach, and his body temperature began to rise. Something was not right.

"Manny, wake up…can you hear me?" he whispered a little louder.

Still, no reply.

He bravely pulled the covers from over his head, stopping midway at his nose. A wuthering breeze rippled across his face, startling him. He quickly pulled the blanket back over his head. Then in a small corner of his mind, he heard his mother's voice in a whisper.

"Pray that evil away. That's the only thing that roams in the middle of the night. Do not acknowledge. Do not listen to it. Pray it away." Her voice hypnotized him and gained total dominance over his mind. Lost in a trance, he began whispering to himself.

"I plead the blood of Christ over my life. I plead the blood of Christ over my life."

Jean-Jacques's eyes reappeared, fixed on the ceiling fan that did not move, as his body trembled with anxiety because he couldn't remember what he thought last. The room boiled like the last month of summer. It was the type of scorching heat that opened the pores on his skin. He gazed over at Emmanuel's bed. He could see the outline of his silhouette tucked underneath his covers. He pulled off one of his socks and launched it over toward his bed. It bounced off his body, but there was no movement. Unexpectedly, the curtains next to Emmanuel's bed fluttered in the air. Jean-Jacques rolled onto his stomach and pressed his face into the mattress. He held his breath as he pretended that he disappeared into the bed.

*Why would the window be unlocked this time of the morning?* he thought. Had someone broken in? They had never slept with the bedroom window unbolted. Their mother checked before bed every night. Although physically removed from crime-infested Port-Au-Prince, known as the Lower Ninth Ward, her memories of being raised there remained.

Life was supposed to be safer in Bywater, their mother said. Much better than the poverty-stricken Port-au-Prince, where they secretly moved from. Jean-Jacques anticipated Emmanuel's scream for help. Nothing. He slowly turned his head back toward the window with one eye open. Emmanuel remained peacefully sleep in his bed. He glanced at the alarm clock; an hour had passed. Tired of being ignored, Jean-Jacques decided to take the matter into his own hands. He slowly scooted to the edge of the bed, careful not to make the bedsprings squeak too loudly. He slid his feet to the floor and dug the tips of his toes deep into the innermost layer of the damp carpet. There was no other movement in the room except for the curtains dancing wildly in the air. He inhaled a deep breath of air with his eyes focused on Emmanuel's bed.

"Be brave at all times. Be brave even in the darkness, for there is nothing to fear but the hesitation right before you move your feet. Be brave," he murmured the mantra Emmanuel had taught him when he was younger. His mind raced back and forth, tapping the pedal of his courage, igniting the flames of his fearlessness. He counted down backward on his fingers: five, four, three, two, one.

He dashed across the room, crashing into the bottom rail of Emmanuel's bed. He tumbled to the floor and curled up in the fetal position with one hand over his mouth and the other on his toe. His mother was sure to walk into the room after the commotion. He swallowed the pain, hurried to his knees, and pulled himself up onto Emmanuel's bed.

"Manny." He nudged him a little. "Manny, say something."

He nervously pulled the comforter from over Emmanuel's head, shocked at what he saw. His eyes darted around the room in confusion as he rubbed the back of his neck. Where was Emmanuel? His body had been replaced by pillows stacked one on top of the other. Jean-Jacques threw the pillows onto the floor and moved his hand savagely up and down the bedspread in the hope that Emmanuel would somehow appear like a magic trick.

He hurried over to the bedroom door, grabbed the moist doorknob, and gently opened it, careful not to make any unusual noise that would wake their mother. He poked his head in the hallway. No strange sound or movement could be heard, just the smoke detector in need of a new battery. He quietly closed the door and leaned against the wall. His eyes drifted to the shoe rack that sat behind the bedroom door. Emmanuel's favorite pair of sneakers were gone.

Had Emmanuel finally gained the courage to run away like he'd always planned, like he'd always mumbled under his breath?

"I hate it here. I can't wait till I go live with my father."

No one hated Bywater more than Emmanuel. He was the black sheep of the neighborhood. His skin color drew suspicion everywhere he went. The neighbors whispered among each other.

"Who is that family that lives in that house on Monday Street? The mother with the cute little boy and the ugly one. How'd they afford that house?"

Valerie was aware of the stares and rumors that made her even more self-conscious, causing her to leave Emmanuel in the car whenever they shopped at the local stores. His dark skin could not be hidden as much as Valerie had so often prayed for, even taking the matter into her own hands when God had not answered. Anyone could understand if he had run away and escaped the torment he received daily.

But Emmanuel had promised to take Jean-Jacques with him if he ever did run away. Jean-Jacques should have known better. Emmanuel no longer kept promises. There was no longer any brotherly love shared between the two. Emmanuel had changed into someone Jean-Jacques no longer recognized, like a childhood friend who moved away. He stared down at his hands, shoulders drooping. The corners of his eyes swelled, and his chest tightened. He examined the empty feeling of the room. What was he going to tell their mother?

Chatter from outside the window interrupted his thoughts. He rushed to the window, expecting to see Emmanuel. He frowned as he wiped his runny nose with the back of his hand.

It was the Fermonts—father, mother, two children, and a dog—all blue-eyed with blond hair, the perfect family. At least that was what Valerie called them. He watched them scurry back and forth, in and out of their home, loading their family van. Their dog barked at the sky as they stepped on the gas pedal and sped out of the driveway.

"Good! I hope they never come back!"

Jean-Jacques thought. They were the ones who always called the police whenever they saw Emmanuel outside. They thought that because he was black, he had to be up to no good, even it was checking the mailbox. They were the noisiest and unfriendliest of their neighbors, with their genetically modified smiles and robotic hellos.

Jean-Jacques stared up at the sky. It was hard to tell night from the day. An overcast sky had hovered over the city for six days already. He pushed down on the window, but it would not close. To his surprise, stuck in between, holding the shutter open, was his missing black obsidian crystal. One of many he had stolen from his Granme's home. He struggled to remove it, but it would not budge. Emmanuel was gone, the window was open, and an evil omen was stuck in between as Valerie would say. What was he to tell her? Exhausted by the unfortunate events, Jean-Jacques turned away from the window. He was at a crossroads. Then, out of nowhere, the unimaginable thought arose within him. Something he had always wanted to do. He had no other choice. The energy in the room turned dark, but he was unafraid. He walked to the closet, hands shaking as he opened the doors. He took a deep breath and crawled in. There was no turning back. His heartbeat increased at the very thought of what he was about to do. Something he had never done before but read about in the books at his Granme's home. He reached the back of the closet and sat with his legs intertwined, Indian style. He moved aside a shoebox that sat in the corner, filled with awards that Emmanuel had received throughout the years but had gone unnoticed. Jean-Jacques removed a piece of sheetrock from the wall and confidently reached inside, pulling out a black wooden box with a goat head carved on top. He closed his eyes and calmed his breath before opening it.

He pulled out a small picture of an old man with a top hat and a little puppy standing directly behind him. The photo caused a fluttering in his stomach. He then pulled out a small piece of red cloth, followed by a white candle, two pieces of peppermint candy, three pennies, and a set of bronze skeleton keys. All items he had stolen from his Granme's home also. He placed them all neatly on top of the red cloth. He grabbed the white candle and, with his fingernail, carved: "Bring Emmanuel home!" He lit the wick, his hands shivering. He closed his eyes and repeated the words he had remembered from the book: "Ase Ase Papa Legba open the way." He repeated the words over and over until his eyes hung low, and his words drifted into silence.

# 3

## I BEAT YOU BECAUSE I

## LOVE YOU

*Love is or love ain't. Thin love ain't love at all.*
**TONI MORRISON**

Emmanuel jumped over the fence to his backyard. It was the break of dawn with an overcast sky. Five days had gone by with not one ray of sun. It was hard to tell night from day. The wind howled through the trees, and their branches waved back and forth, deposing their dead leaves. The fallen leaves blew across Emmanuel's face. The hair on his arms stood up. He hurried to the window, relieved that the crystal was still there. He removed the crystal and placed it in his pocket, then quietly slipped through the window, head-first, unaware that the obsidian crystal had fallen from his pocket. He backed away from the window and stumbled over his pillows. Emmanuel jumped to his feet, shaken. He bolted over to Jean-Jacques's bed, greeted only by the foul stench of urine that arose from the sheets. His heart plummeted to this stomach.

"Jean-Jacques, where are you?" Emmanuel whispered through his teeth as he spun around the room in a circle. A faintness came over him.

He slapped his forehead with the palm of his hand, thinking: *Where could Jean-Jacques be at this time of the morning?* Emmanuel bolted over to the bedroom door. He reached into the buckle of his pants and pulled out the flashlight. Emmanuel slowly cracked the door open and flashed the light down the dark, seemingly endless hallway. No sign of Jean-Jacques. Emmanuel shut the door and searched around the room. A gleam of light appeared in the corner of his eye, coming from underneath the closet door. Sweat spouted in the palm of his hand, and his fingers tingled.

"Jean-Jacques, that better be you!" Emmanuel moved toward the closet door with the flashlight raised above his head. He opened the door, and the flashlight dropped out of his hand. A sinister smirk came across his face at the thought of Valerie actually witnessing her precious Jean-Jacques unearthing the hidden family legacy. The one secret that she desperately tried to hide; but everyone knows that you do not choose voodoo, it chooses you.

As much as he resented his mother, Emmanuel knew the consequences Jean-Jacques would face if Valerie discovered him practicing voodoo. That he would be left alone with Father Silas to pray and cleanse him of any demonic spirits. Emmanuel blew the candles out and quickly threw all of the strange items into the mysterious box, then placed it back in its hidden place.

"Wake up! Come on! Get up!" Emmanuel shook Jean-Jacques's shoulders. A slight moan came from Jean-Jacques's mouth as he rose from his slumped posture.

"Where am I?" Jean-Jacques asked, wiping his eyes. Emmanuel covered Jean-Jacques's mouth.

"Shhh. Be quiet. Just come on. We don't have a lot of time," Emmanuel replied, exiting the closet. Jean-Jacques crawled out of the closet.

Emmanuel was at the dresser, shirtless. He placed the blue bandana inside the bottom drawer along with the notebook.

"Manny, will those scars ever go away on your back?" Jean-Jacques asked.

Then, there, the disturbing memory arose in Emmanuel's mind of how those scars became embroidered on the top of his skin.

It was Jean-Jacques's fault that Emmanuel even had those scars, which had occurred after their mother discovered a mojo bag in the home once.

Valerie had stormed into their room, holding both a Bible and an extension cord in one hand and dangling the mojo bag in the other.

"What is this? Who had this?" Valerie opened the small black fennel bag and tossed the roots on the floor. "How did this get inside my home?" she shouted.

Jean-Jacques looked at Emmanuel. That was all Valerie needed. Emmanuel shrugged his shoulders and looked away. Valerie fired the mojo bag at Emmanuel, hitting him across the head.

"You tryin' to mess with me, huh? Answer me! You trying to put roots on me? You always up to no good!" Valerie screamed.

"It's not mine," Emmanuel explained. He cut his eyes away, searching for Jean-Jacques.

"Look at me when I'm talking to you." Valerie slapped Emmanuel across the face.

Emmanuel looked her dead in the eye, and the words spilled out like venom. "I *said*…it's not *mine*!" Valerie slapped him again.

"Who do you think you're talking to? Strip. Take your clothes off!"

Emmanuel stripped down to his underwear. Valerie shoved the Bible in Emmanuel's hand. "Open it to 2 Leviticus 20:27."

Emmanuel calmly opened the Bible.

"Hurry up!" Valerie rushed him.

Emmanuel stopped, then pointed his finger directly on the Bible verse. He mumbled the words under his breath.

The extension cord pierced down across Emmanuel's back. The Bible dropped from his hand.

"Did you just throw the Bible on the floor?" Valerie asked.

"No. No, ma'am," Emmanuel answered as he nervously bent down to grab the Bible, eyes focused on the extension cord dangling from Valerie's hand.

Another lash came down across his back.

"Next one: 2 Chronicles 33:6, and this time you better speak up!" Valerie roared.

With every Bible verse shouted, the lash

pressed upon Emmanuel's memory, an agonizing pain he would never forget. He watched Valerie's hand until she finally dropped the extension cord to the floor, out of breath. He kept his eyes low, glued to the text of the Bible, unsure what was to come next. He could feel the heat from Valerie's breathing pouring down on him with such vitriol. He waited, frozen in place, afraid to move until Valerie walked out of the room.

Emmanuel turned around from the dresser. His and Jean-Jacques's eyes met again like that unforgettable night.

"What are you staring at?" asked Emmanuel as he changed back into his pajamas." Emmanuel walked to over Jean-Jacques's bed.

"You smell that?" Emmanuel asked.

Jean-Jacques covered his pajama pants with his hand.

"Yeah, you wet the bed again, pissy pants. Way to go!" Emmanuel shoved Jean-Jacques out of the way.

Jean-Jacques turned away and changed

his pajamas. Emmanuel cleaned the room for anything that might be out of place. He flipped Jean-Jacques's mattress over to hide the smell of urine and changed the sheets. They both climbed into their beds just before Valerie's alarm clock went off.

# 4

## UNPLANNED PARENTHOOD

*You wanna fly, you got to give up the*
*shit that weighs you down.*

**TONI MORRISON**

Valerie was not the type of woman to lie
around all morning, but on this morning she
retreated from her day. She pressed the snooze
button on the alarm clock and did not immediately rise to greet the day as she usually did.
She removed her sleep mask, then gazed at the
light that sat at the bottom of her bedroom
door. It gave the room a bit of hope, but she
turned away, rolled over, and exhaled. Like all
residents of Crescent City, the one question

that lingered in her mind was either stay or go. She thought about what all had to be done if she did decide to leave: pack up all of her boys' clothes, pick up all of her clothes, then gather the essential things in the house and pack them up, too. The list when on and on and on. She grew tired from the thought of it all. But how could she leave? The life she tirelessly worked to build, piece by piece, for her boys was in Bywater. It was everything she once wanted. A suburban crime-free community with no hoodlums walking around with their pants sagging low. No trash-filled streets that concealed the beauty of the neighborhood. Manicured lawns taken care of by the homeowners association. Sidewalks filled with innocent blond and brunette children who rode their bikes without adult supervision. Joggers who ran at the break of the morning and, most importantly, no police or ambulance sirens that wailed at godawful hours of the night.

The alarm clock went off for a second time.

Valerie pulled her breath in and exhaled as she rose to grab her cell phone to check the weather. She slid on her slippers, wrapped herself in her robe, and walked to the bedroom window. She pulled apart the curtains, lit a cigarette, then cracked the window open just enough to blow the smoke out. From her bedroom window, she could see Port-au-Prince. She was distant but not as far away as she would have hoped.

Valerie lived hidden on the edge of a new world, in a community of faces that looked nothing like hers, but in her mind, everyone did. Like most Creole women in the South, Valerie wasn't necessarily white or black but a mixture of sorts. Early on, she learned that it was better to appear as white as possible than to live with the burden of being black. With a stroke of a makeup brush, she taught herself how to erase any feature that was too ethnic. She had learned how to make her skin appear lighter, her lips thinner, and the tip of her nose smaller. She replaced her natural grey eyes with blue contacts and also straightened her curly hair every three days, never forgetting to hide the baby hairs that slept, curled up at the edges of her forehead.

Her new adopted identity masked the pain she carried for being teased as a child by darker-skinned girls whom she had once admired. The taunting of being called a "voodoo child" because of her mother's spiritual practice no longer echoed in her mind whenever she painted her face on. She no longer heard the neighborhood children's voices that once teased her about the clothes she wore and her untamed curly hair that smelled of patchouli oil and burnt sage. Valerie was no longer the girl who everyone teased and bullied as a child. She was now beautiful enough to capture any man's attention, even her married boss, who frequented her home after work hours.

Her life was almost as perfect as she'd dreamed. Then the thought arose within her like a flame: how free life would be without her children, especially Emmanuel, whose skin color she could not hide. It was silly of her to think that because she was fair skinned that Emmanuel would take her complexion. The truth was she felt trapped being Emmanuel's mother but never told a soul, not even God. She had been a happy woman before meeting Emmanuel's father, the first man she loved and the first man to leave her stranded as a single mother. The very thought of Emmanuel evoked a feeling of rejection. She resented her firstborn, who, in her mind, just had to be adopted, and that is what she told everyone she met who questioned her about him.

Then there was Jean-Jacques, the perfect child, from his skin complexion to his curly red hair, down to the freckles painted across his nose. Jean-Jacques was indeed her golden child. But still, deep down inside, Valerie knew that being a mother was something she never wanted for herself. The truth was Valerie was tired of running from her past, tired of motherhood, and tired of putting everyone before herself. She was tired of pretending that everything was perfect.

Valerie rubbed the middle of her forehead, trying to erase the thoughts that eroded her mind. There again was that feeling of freedom haunting her, making its presence known. All of her selfish wants, needs, and what a new life could feel like if she abandoned her responsibilities and left Crescent City was standing at the doorstep of her mind, awaiting an invite. For once, she wanted to breathe, live her life for herself, and start over. In her mind, God might have finally answered her prayers with Hurricane Katrina. She flicked her cigarette out the window and walked to her bedroom door.

"Jean-Jacques! Emmanuel! Time to get up!" she yelled.

# 5

## BLOOD BROTHERS

*God blesses him who helps his brother.*

**ABU BAKR**

Jean-Jacques and Emmanuel both jumped up from their beds from the sound of Valerie's footsteps. They could tell she had a lot on her mind.

"Get on your knees. Hurry!" Emmanuel whispered to Jean-Jacques.

Emmanuel closed his eyes and placed his hands in prayer position. Just as Jean-Jacques was about to close his eyes, too, he spotted his obsidian crystal lying on the floor in clear view.

"Manny...look," Jean-Jacques whispered, shooting his eyes toward the misplaced object.

They both stared at each other. It was too late. Emmanuel closed his eyes, hoping Valerie did not see the crystal while Jean-Jacques launched a pillow across the room, landing precisely on top of his target. Emmanuel had begun whispering the morning prayer just before Valerie walked through the bedroom door.

"Dear Christ, our God, thank you for allowing us to see another day. We are here to serve you, and only you, Christ our God. You are the master, and we are your sheep. Our every footstep will follow you, all the days of our life, Christ our God. We surrender our will to you, and only you, Christ our God. We cast out any desires that do not serve you, Christ our God. Amen."

Jean-Jacques opened his eyes. Valerie was sitting on the edge of his bed.

"Good morning, sweet face." Valerie kissed him on the cheek.

Emmanuel got up from his knees.

"Good morning," he said in a muffled voice.

Valerie cut her eyes at him. Her smile faded to stone.

"Why is this room so dirty? Did I raise you to live in filth?" she asked, looking at Emmanuel.

Emmanuel began to make his bed. "No, ma'am." Cleanliness is next to godliness," he replied, sarcastically mocking her gestures.

Valerie began making her way toward the window. She rested one hand on her chin and the other on her hip.

"That's odd. I could have sworn I locked this window last night," she stated to herself, tapping her fingers on her chin.

She locked the window, then turned around to both Jean-Jacques and Emmanuel with one eyebrow raised. They made no eye contact and continued making their beds.

"Yes, cleanliness is next to godliness, but I would advise you to watch your tone when you speak to me, Emmanuel," she continued as she bent down to grab Jean-Jacques's pillow off the floor. Emmanuel quickly ran over and placed his hand on top of the pillow.

"I got it, Ma," he said.

"Ma! I am not your Ma. I am your mother." Valerie grabbed Emmanuel by the chin.

"How many times do I have to tell you about using that kind of language in this house? What happened to your face?" She turned Emmanuel's face from side to side.

Emmanuel pinched his lips and cut his eyes away, staring at the wall.

"I know you hear me talking to you. Was it those same boys from Port-Au-Prince?" she continued.

"What do you care?" Emmanuel mumbled.

"Who in the hell do you think you are talking to, huh?" Valerie slapped him across the face.

"You little, ungrateful, disrespectful bastard. I asked you a question," she continued.

"Mother, your phone is ringing," Jean-Jacques chimed in.

Valerie shoved Emmanuel's face away.

"Fine. Don't tell me. But whatever happens in the darkness shall come to light. Get up off the floor. I don't care about the weather reports. You and Jean-Jacques are still going to church. Now clean up this room and get dressed."

Valerie rolled her shoulders back and tightened her robe. She looked about the room one last time, then strutted out of the bedroom door.

"I hate her!" Emmanuel whispered underneath his breath.

Jean-Jacques walked over to the pillow and lifted it up.

"Where is it? Give it to me. Where is my crystal?" he demanded of Emmanuel.

"Move out of my way. I don't know what you're talking about, I don't have no stupid rock," Emmanuel replied, shoving Jean-Jacques out of the way.

"It's not a stupid rock. It's a magic crystal, and I've been looking for it; now give it to me,"

Jean-Jacques demanded, reaching for Emmanuel's pajama pants.

"Well, I don't care what you call it. I don't have it. You must have dreamt it," Emmanuel stated, shrugging the question away.

"I saw it in the window. When you were gone. Give it to me, or I'm going to tell mother you snuck out of the house," Jean-Jacques charged.

"Go right ahead and tell her, so I can show her what you were doing in the closet," Emmanuel challenged as he walked over to the closet door and opened it.

"Who do you think cleaned up your little ritual? Who is always cleaning up your messes? Did you think it just magically disappeared when you woke?" Emmanuel asked.

Jean-Jacques walked over to the closet and looked inside. His secret was exposed. There was nothing he could say.

"I put everything back right there." Emmanuel continued pointing at the wall's hidden spot. "Papa Legbra...PAPA LEGBRA. Why would you bring a picture of Papa Legbra into this house? Do you know what would happen if Mother saw that? You heard the tales about Papa Legbra, right?" Emmanuel asked.

"Yeah. So? I'm not scared," Jean-Jacques answered.

"Well you need to be! Don't you know, the more you start to believe in that stuff… the more likely bad things start to happen," Emmanuel said.

"None of the bad stuff is true," Jean-Jacques countered.

"How do you know?" Emmanuel asked.

"I read about it in a book at Granme's house," Jean-Jacques replied.

"Well, keep believing in it if you want to, and people will one day think you are crazy, just like Granme," Emmanuel declared.

"Why did you take my crystal if you don't believe in it?" Jean-Jacques asked.

"Enough about the stupid crystal. Look, if you don't say anything about me sneaking out of the house, then I won't say anything about your little ritual, ok?" Emmanuel proposed.

"Fine...I won't say anything," Jean-Jacques agreed.

"Ok, good. Now go on, put your church clothes on before Mother comes in here again," Emmanuel responded.

# 6

## DARK CLOUDS

*In search of my mother's garden, I found my own.*

**ALICE WALKER**

Jean-Jacques and Emmanuel sat across from each other on each end of the living room couch, patiently waiting for the church van to arrive. Emmanuel flicked through the television, annoyed that every channel was hijacked by the news reporting the most massive hurricane to hit Crescent City, Hurricane Katrina. Jean-Jacques hopped off the couch and strolled down the hallway to their mother's bedroom. He peeked through the crack of her bedroom door.

"Mother, may I come in?" he whispered, pushing the door open.

"What did I tell you about coming into my room without knocking first?" Valerie asked.

"Sorry, ma'am," Jean-Jacques responded, then paused, staring at her empty vanity. All of her makeup, face creams, and countless bottles of perfume were gone. Valerie stood in the doorway of her closet, shoving her luggage out of view.

"Did you boys clean your room and make your beds?" she asked.

"Yes, ma'am," he responded, his eyes peering around the bedroom, never before seeing her room unkempt. "Why are all of your things thrown around? Are you coming to church with us?" he continued.

"What did I tell you about asking so many questions?" she responded. Valerie walked over to him and bent down. "Did you wash your face?" she asked.

"Yes, ma'am!" he responded, nodding while staring past her into the closet at the empty luggage on the floor.

"Look at me. What's wrong? Something's on your mind," she asked, grabbing his hand.

Jean-Jacques looked down at the floor.

"Are you afraid because of all that talk about the hurricane? That's nothing your little heart should be worried about, you hear? That's why I'm sending you to church. Christ has not given us the spirit of fear, but…what?" she asked.

"Faith," Jean-Jacques answered. "How come you don't come to church with us anymore? How come you always send us on the church van?"

"What did I tell you about asking too many questions?" Valerie stood up and tightened her robe. "If it weren't for those messy church wives, I'd be right there with you," she responded, caressing her hair as she walked to her bedroom window.

"The church van is here!" Emmanuel yelled from the living room.

Valerie pointed to the door. "Go on now. Behave and listen to what Father Silas has to say."

Jean-Jacques walked to the bedroom door, then froze. He turned around and glanced at his mother one more time while she gazed out of the bedroom window. The church van honked again.

He hurried down the hall and bolted out the front door. He climbed up the church van's stairs only to be met with squinted eyes from the few old women in the van.

"What were you doing?" asked Emmanuel.

"Nothing. I forgot something," Jean-Jacques replied.

There were fewer people in the van than usual. Usually, the women babbled about church activities, and a few of them even gossiped about other members. But no one spoke a word; everyone just sat and stared out the windows. Crossing the bridge into Port-au-Prince was something both Jean-Jacques and Emmanuel looked forward to. It was the only day they ever got to visit their old neighborhood. There was no place in Crescent City like Port-au-Prince. One could never forget the aroma. The early-morning air filled their noses with lively scents of grilled onions, pungent spices, and the salty charred swine that they could taste in their mouths without a bite.

Driving through the pothole-filled streets was like riding a rollercoaster. Then there were the old abandoned business buildings, hunched over like widows praying for the return of their deceased loved ones. One could never forget the people waiting at bus stops, their faces carrying half-smiles, neither happy nor sad. It seemed the weight of the world sat on their shoulders. The only change Port-au-Prince had seen over the past generations was the seasons, but still, it was somehow magical. The residents walked about with a rhythm that could only be felt. The language, however broken, could be understood by the facial expression that followed. Life in Port-au-Prince was what it was, and the people had grown to accept that it was a world of its own.

The church van pulled into the empty parking lot.

"Where is everyone? I tell ya, these people don't have faith in Christ like they used to," said one of the church ladies.

"I survived Hurricane Betsy in nineteen-sixty-five. I ain't scared of no Katrina," said another one.

"Amen to that, Sista!" shouted one more as they headed up the church stairs. Emmanuel and Jean-Jacques followed behind.

Jean-Jacques's eyes were glued to the gargoyles that hung from the side of the church building. "Manny, look, I think they've moved since the last time."

"You say that every Sunday. Shut up and come on," Emmanuel responded while he held the door open for Jean-Jacques.

The main lobby was at the calmest it had ever been. The few church members in attendance all just stood around looking at one another until the sanctuary doors opened. Emmanuel grabbed Jean-Jacques's hand, directing him to a seat not too far in the back but also not too close to the altar.

"Sit here. Do not move. I'll be back right back," Emmanuel directed.

"Where are you going? I want to go with you," Jean-Jacques said.

"Just to the restroom. I'll be back. Stay put, okay?" Emmanuel asked.

"Okay. But don't take too long," Jean-Jacques answered while he folded his arms and slid down on the pew.

Once again, Jean-Jacques found himself alone, but not entirely. His eyes were drawn to the giant crucifix that towered over the pulpit. Then the realization dawned on him once again that he felt no connection to the pale-face, blue-eyed, blond-haired man that hung so helplessly. Every emotion he was ever taught to think about the Christ evaporated at that very moment. No feeling of guilt. No sadness. No fear of hell. Nothing.

*How could someone who couldn't save himself save me?* Jean-Jacques thought. This awareness both frightened and liberated him at the same time.

Then out of the quietness of the sanctuary, a small commotion erupted.

"What in the Christ is *she* doing here?!" one member shouted.

Jean-Jacques turned around to the back of the church. His mouth dropped.

"Granme?" he mouthed.

Church members gathered to their feet. By the tone of the church members, Jean-Jacques could tell she was not welcome. He quickly ducked underneath the pew and watched her feet glide down the aisle as if she was floating on a cloud, filling the sanctuary with her herbaceous scent. He rose onto his knees and peeked over the pew once she passed by. She stopped directly in front of the altar. The church members all gasped.

"Leave, you ole voodoo devil. You know you don't belong here!" one yelled.

His Granme looked up at the crucifix that towered over her. With boldness, she walked up the few steps and to the pulpit.

"Why you coming to start trouble? Go on

now. This here's a holy place. Your kind isn't welcome," shouted an old lady from the pews.

Jean-Jacques watched as she reached into her bag and retrieved a small glass jar. She pulled the lid off and then dipped the jar into the bowl of holy water and filled it up. The church members were too afraid to go near her but continued with their insults. She put the lid on the container and then left peacefully out of side exit doors.

*What is Granme up to, and where is she headed?* Jean-Jacques thought.

He rose to his feet. Emmanuel still had not returned, and Jean-Jacques could not contain his curiosity. He quietly slipped out the sanctuary doors unnoticed. His Granme was nowhere in sight, but her voice could be heard coming from the church cemetery. He trotted down the steep path, covering his face from the aggressive wind. Jean-Jacques wandered inside the cemetery roaming past the tall whitewashed mausoleum tombs until he stumbled upon his Granme sitting on a bench, alone, carrying on with laughter and chatter. Just when Jean-Jacques was about to make his presence known, Emmanuel called his name from behind.

"Jean-Jacques! Bro, what are you doing? I have been looking everywhere for you," Emmanuel shouted. "I thought I told you to stay put."

"I…I…I did but—" Jean-Jacques stuttered. "Granme is over there," he continued pointing toward the bench.

"What are you talking about?" Emmanuel asked. "No one is there."

Jean-Jacques turned around, baffled.

"I swear she was there. I'm telling the truth. I saw—" Jean-Jacques tried.

"Forget it. I don't want to hear it," Emmanuel interrupted. "Mother is outside, waiting."

"Huh? Mother? No, she's not. She said the church wives don't like her. That's why she doesn't come to church anymore!" Jean-Jacques argued.

"Just be quiet and come on," Emmanuel insisted.

He grabbed Jean-Jacques's hand, and they quickly traveled back up to the church and into the sanctuary.

"Where is everyone?" Jean-Jacques asked.

"I don't know. They were all gone when I came back. I had to call Mother," Emmanuel answered as he turned to Jean-Jacques.

"Before we head outdoors, I don't want you to be surprised. I called my dad also. He is outside. I'm leaving with him," Emmanuel said.

Jean-Jacques's eyes squished together. He grabbed Emmanuel's arm. "Huh? Well, I'm going, too," he demanded.

"You can't come with me. He's not your father. You have to stay with Mother," Emmanuel responded while he reached into his pocket. "I have something for you." He pulled out the obsidian crystal. "Here is your crystal, but don't get caught with it."

"Why did you take it in the first place?" Jean-Jacques asked.

"You left it out one day in the closet, so I took it. Not to save you, but to save me from getting a beating," Emmanuel explained. "Now, put it deep in your pocket, and don't let it fall out. Oh, and one last thing. When Mother asks—because she will—what Father Silas's sermon was about...just say Matthew 18:10-13, the Wandering Sheep. She won't ask any questions after that. Okay? You got it?"

For the first time in a long time, Jean-Jacques felt that brotherly bond he and Emmanuel once had.

"Matthew 18:10-13, the Wandering Sheep. Okay. I got it," Jean-Jacques repeated the command back to Emmanuel, then placed the crystal in his pocket. He looked back at the crucifix as they walked out of the sanctuary doors.

"Boy, get in the car. What were you doing? We have to get going," Valerie shouted from her car. She rushed over and grabbed

Jean-Jacques's hand. Emmanuel's father was there waiting, too. Jean-Jacques climbed in the backseat of their mother's vehicle while Emmanuel went to his father's car. Valerie got in the car.

"Where is Emmanuel going?" Jean-Jacques asked in a tearful, broken voice.

"What did I tell you about asking so many questions? Don't say another word until we get to where we are going," Valerie demanded.

Jean-Jacques reached into his pocket and felt for the crystal; he waved to Emmanuel. Emmanuel waved back, then pressed his index finger to his lips.

# 7

## BROKEN CROWN

---

*It is not light that we need, but fire; it is not
the gentle shower, but thunder. We need the
storm, the whirlwind, and the earthquake.*

**FREDERICK DOUGLASS**

Jean-Jacques watched Valerie turn from one
radio station to the next, and every station
reported the same warning: Evacuate! Evacuate! Evacuate!

"Where are we going?" Jean-Jacques asked,
folding his arms across his chest, visibly upset
that he could not go with Emmanuel.

Valerie turned down the radio, ignoring
Jean-Jacques's question.

She reached into the glove compartment, grabbed a cigarette, lit it, exhaled, then quickly glanced at him in the review mirror.

"What did Father Silas discuss in the church today?" Valerie asked, breaking the awkward silence.

Jean-Jacques's mind drew a blank; all he could think about was Granme and the cemetery.

"Boy, I know you heard me." Valerie flicked her cigarette butt out the window. "What was Father Silas's sermon about?"

Without much effort, Jean-Jacques's thoughts spilled from his mouth.

"Granme. Granme was at church today," he answered, looking her firmly in the eye, knowing the name would strike a nerve.

Valerie slammed on brakes. Her eyes now frowned and lips tightened.

"Jean-Jacques, you just left the church. What did I tell you about lying?" she responded.

"I'm not! She was there! I saw Granme!" Jean-Jacques continued.

"Did your brother put you up to saying this? I know he did. Just sit back and be quiet!"

Valerie grabbed the steering wheel with both hands, her eyes twitched.

"Where are we going?" Jean-Jacques asked again.

Valerie turned around. "What did I tell you about asking so many questions?"

Jean-Jacques reached into his pocket to feel for the crystal, then remembered the Bible verse Emmanuel mentioned.

"Matthew 18:10-13. The Wandering Sheep," Jean-Jacques blurted out loud.

"Huh? What did you say?" Valerie asked as she turned around, looking him directly in the eyes.

Jean-Jacques swallowed, then resumed, "That's what Father Silas talked about. Matthew 18:10-13, the Wandering Sheep," he quoted.

Valerie turned around toward the steering wheel, then spoke the Bible verse out loud.

Matthew 18:10-13

10 "See that you do not despise one of these little ones. For I tell you that their angels in heaven always see the face of my Father in heaven." [11] [a]

12 "What do you think? If a man owns a hundred sheep, and one of them wanders away, will he not leave the ninety-nine on the hills and go to look for the one that wandered off?" 13 "And if he finds it, truly I tell you, he is happier about that one sheep than about the ninety-nine that did not wander off."

Valerie combed her fingers through her hair and exhaled.

"Jean-Jacques, if you could be a sheep or a goat, which one would you be?" she asked.

Jean-Jacques paused and thought about the question. The apparent answer to appease Valerie would be to say sheep, but deep down within himself, Jean-Jacques knew that he was no sheep, no follower, and disliked being controlled or told what to do.

"It's okay. Don't lie. You just left the church," Valerie encouraged him.

"A goat," he boldly answered. "Wild and free!"

Valerie bit her lip, then reached into the glove compartment and grabbed another cigarette.

The palms of Jean-Jacques's hands began to sweat, watching her talk to herself. He looked out the window, seeing the levee that protected Port-au-Prince from the Mississippi River.

"Is this the way to Granme's house? Are we going to Granme's house?" he asked.

"Be quiet. You've said enough today," Valerie responded.

The car suddenly stopped, not in front of Granme's house but a few houses down. Jean-Jacques said nothing. He watched Valerie thump her fingers on the steering wheel. She then unbuckled her seatbelt and got out of the car, opening his door.

"Why are we here at Granme's house?" Jean-Jacque asked.

"What did I tell you about asking so many

questions?" Valerie replied. She grabbed a small duffle bag from the trunk of the car.

"I need you to take this bag up to Granme's house, okay? I'm going to wait in the car for you," she directed.

Jean-Jacques scratched at his cheeks and then both temples. He grabbed the bag from his mother's trembling hands.

"What's in the bag? Does Granme know I'm coming?" Jean-Jacques asked.

"What did I tell you about asking too many questions? Go on now," Valerie insisted, shooing him away.

Jean-Jacques began the long, drawn-out walk up to his Granme's home until his mother's car was no longer in view. Granme was the family living legend. Her life was much different from the world Jean-Jacques was taught. To any believer of Christ, she lived a sinful life. Her battered antebellum home lay tucked away and closed off from the outside world. Few people bothered her: only those who believed in the magic of voodoo and her faithful devotees visited. Jean-Jacques had not been to visit since that night on St. John's Eve and was not sure what to expect. He arrived at the large wooden front door, which was slightly cracked open.

"Granme, is that you?" he asked.

He pushed the door open and continued inside, dropping the duffle bag at the front door.

"Granme, it's me, Jean-Jacques," he echoed.

The old home was nearly empty inside, much different from what he remembered. The furniture was covered with white sheets. The plants that once hung from the ceiling were gone. The many wall paintings of the Orishas had been taken down. Then, out of nowhere, Jean-Jacques heard the sounds of beating drums coming from down the hall.

"Granme...is that you? Where are you?" he asked again.

He traveled to where the sounds were coming from, and with each step, the sounds grew louder. He found himself in front of his

Granme's secret chamber, the place she kept all of the spells, potions, magic books, and creepy concoctions. Jean-Jacques had only been inside it once, when he stole the obsidian crystal.

He placed his ear to the door.

"Granme, you in there?" he whispered.

He then bent down and peeked under the door. Then suddenly the front door slammed shut, frightening him to his feet.

"Jean-Jacques, what do you think you're doing?" she asked.

His Granme was standing with both hands on her hips. As far as he knew, Granme was the oldest person in Port-au-Prince. She was quite unusual, nothing like anyone else who lived there. Her eyes spoke of worlds unseen to the human eye.

He hurried to the front door and into her arms. "Hey, Granme. I have something to give you." Jean-Jacques grabbed the duffle bag from the floor and handed it to her.

"I have to hurry back to the car. Mother is waiting for me," he explained.

"You think your mother is out there waiting for you?" she asked with a chuckle.

Granme handed Jean-Jacques back the duffle bag.

"Do me a favor and open it for me. Go on. Look inside," she insisted.

Jean-Jacques opened the bag, and there he came to find his toothbrush, some underwear, and a few articles of clothing. It was true: his mother had left him. His shoulders sank, and his eyes went dull.

"Why is my stuff in here, Granme?" he asked.

Granme lifted his chin. "Aw, now, don't you go being sad. You are right where you belong. Now come on and follow me. I want to show you something," she said.

Jean-Jacques zipped the duffle bag closed and followed Granme through the kitchen and out the backdoor. She stood on the porch with both hands on her hips, staring up at the sky. Then she stepped down into her garden. Jean-Jacques followed. The once flourishing garden full of herbs, plants, and vegetables was nearly empty.

"Granme…can I ask you something? Where is everything? All of your stuff…in the house and here…in the garden…are you leaving too…like everyone else?" Jean-Jacques asked.

He watched as she got down on her knees, digging a small hole in the soil.

He rubbed the back of his neck, confused.

She then got up from her knees and slapped the dust from her hands.

"Take your socks and shoes off, and put your feet in the hole," Granme directed.

Jean-Jacques looked down at the soil. Then back at his Granme, unsure of what was going on.

"Go ahead," she encouraged him.

He moved the dirt around with the tips of his toes, skeptical.

"Boy, you scared of dirt? We don't have all day, Jean-Jacques Dupre," she continued.

"Dupre?" Jean-Jacques paused and look at her. "Dupre is not my name," he replied.

Granme grabbed him up by one arm. "What you do mean Dupre isn't your name? That is your birth name…our legacy. Shame on your mother for telling you anything different. What other name do you have if Dupre isn't your last name?" she asked.

"Jean-Jacques is my name…that's it," he answered, puzzled.

"No, Dupre is your last name," Granme fired back. "Shame on your mother, but that's expected of her. Always wanting to be something other than herself. Jean-Jacques, you come from a bloodline of spiritual warriors that carried that last name. It is not by chance that you are here today, nor is it that you've found interest in the dark side of life. In the darkness is where you find yourself, not in the light. Let me show you something. Go on. Stick your feet in the soil," she instructed.

Jean-Jacques looked back down at the soil. He dug his feet in.

"Do you feel that?" she asked.

"I don't feel anything," he replied.

"Go deeper and close your eyes, and take a deep breath," Granme affirmed.

Jean-Jacques closed his eyes and took a deep breath. Granme stomped on the ground three times with her right foot. Then, in the darkness of the soil, ignited a spark of electric energy that shot up from Jean-Jacques's feet and through his entire body, startling him. He immediately opened his eyes.

"What…what was that Granme?" he stuttered. His whole body was shaking with chills. He quickly removed his feet from the soil and ran back up to the porch.

Granme chuckled. "No need to be afraid. Just like a seed planted in soil awaiting proper nutrients to grow, so is our soul waiting to be acknowledged. To find yourself, you have to return to where you came from," Granme replied as she joined him on the porch. Granme took a seat on the steps of the porch.

"Come here…come sit down and talk to me," she said. Jean-Jacques walked and sat down in-between her legs. Granme then wrapped her arms across his shoulders and pulled him in close.

"I want you to tell me about this dream you've been having," she said.

Jean-Jacques's mouth fell open. He paused to look up at Granme. He had not mentioned the dream to anyone, not even Emmanuel.

"Go on," Granme encouraged, clutching him a little tighter. Her warm embrace assured him that he was safe to speak and that he had nothing to worry about.

Jean-Jacques closed his eyes and bravely revisited the dream that felt more like a nightmare. His eye began to flinch at seeing most of Port-au-Prince underwater. Then his ears flooded with the desperate cries for help from the many stranded people on the Danziger Bridge, with no food, no water, no help. His nose wrinkled as he mentioned the foul stench of human feces and decaying bodies that filled the air for days. Jean-Jacques opened his eyes, startled that the day had turned into night. He turned around to see

Granme standing over him with her hands stretched out.

"Hey, Granme, how come Mother does not want us to come here? How come she hates Port-au-Prince?" he asked.

"Your mother is like most of our people, destroyed from within, walking around with a broken crown looking to be glued and stitched back together again. Some folks are afraid of accepting who they are. So they hide from themselves, but eventually the truth reveals itself one way or another. That is why you are here," she replied. Droplets of rain began to fall to the ground, and the wind picked up. Granme grabbed Jean-Jacques's hand and pulled him up from the steps.

The doorbell rang from inside. "Oh great, my devotees are here," Granme announced with excitement. She hurried inside, and Jean-Jacques followed.

"Get the door, Jean-Jacques, but stay out of their way," she instructed.

Jean-Jacques watched her head into her

sacred room. He then hurried to the front door. "Who is it?" he asked. No one said a thing. He slowly opened the door, and there was a group of strangers draped in all-black cloaks, each holding an offering in their hands, even a small goat.

"Hello, you must be Jean-Jacques Dupre? We are here to see the high priestess. She is expecting us!"

"How do you know my name?" asked Jean-Jacques, puzzled.

"Because tonight is all about you," she replied, pinching his cheeks. Jean-Jacques stepped aside, watching the goat being tied to the front porch railing. The wind began to blow violently.

They all rushed inside. Jean-Jacques closed the door, then turned around. Everyone removed their cloaks and quickly got to work. The women gathered together in the kitchen, bringing to boil a stockpot of water and calling out each ingredient before dumping it in: rosemary for protection, sage for cleansing, and sea salt for grounding. In the living room, the men quickly set up a small altar directly in the center of the room. Then, one by one, the women decorated the altar, filling it with fruit, red roses, whiskey, and picture of a black woman named Madonna. Then, suddenly, the lights blinked on and off. They all paused and looked at each other. The rain started pouring down, beating the top of the roof like marbles to concrete, and the wind blew about a ghostly howl. Jean-Jacques reached into his pocket and felt for the crystal. Two of the women lifted the steaming stockpot off the stove and carried it down the hall to the bathroom, filling the bathtub.

Another woman walked over to Jean-Jacques and handed him an elixir. "Drink," she said. She then covered his eyes with red satin cloth and led him to the bathroom. Jean-Jacques listened and followed without question. Strangely, he felt safe.

The woman removed his clothes, then placed him in the warm bathwater. She mumbled under her breath while scooping water into her palms, pouring it over Jean-Jacques's head. She removed him from the bathtub, dried his body, dressed him in a white robe, and led him back to the living room. Jean-Jacques's blindfold was removed, and he found himself surrounded by everyone, enclosed in a circle. The room was lit by candlelight. One of the men pulled out a drum and began beating the familiar tune Jean-Jacques had heard when he first got to Granme's house. All of the women began chanting in unison.

The circle broke apart, and standing at the altar with her back turned was Granme dressed in a furry red robe with her head covered by a red silk scarf. She turned around, with her eye dilated and a cigar in her mouth. In her hand, Granme took a piece of white chalk and on the floor in front of the altar she drew the symbol of the voodoos, the VeVe, the gateway between worlds. The woman grabbed Jean-Jacques and laid him on top of the drawn image. They then placed a white candle at each corner of the emblem: north, south, east, and west. Jean-Jacques found himself unable to move his body or even speak. As they lit the wick of each candle, the drummer began beating the drum louder. Jean-Jacques observed Granme moving her hips in a snake-like manner to the rhythm of the drum. The room started spinning. His eyes rolled uncontrollably as he fought to remain conscious.

Then, from a dark corner of the room, he could see the goat dragged to the altar. Granme then drank from the whiskey bottle on the altar and spit on the goat. One of the men handled her a sharp blade. The drumbeat grew louder as Granme raised the sharp knife in the air, holding it with both hands. Then, with a quick movement, she came down and severed the head from the goat's body. They all roared loud with praise as they each passed the decapitated animal's head around, sipping the blood that ran from its throat.

Soon after, everyone began shaking, writhing, and jerking back and forth as they danced around Jean-Jacques, spitting the blood from their mouths onto him. The women screamed from their throats, the men from their chests, all in unison, and they danced around wildly like their bodies were overtaken by an unseen presence.

Jean-Jacques could also feel a new identity emerging within himself. His eyes rolled into the darkness of his mind, only to be awakened by the sound of an explosion. Suddenly the whole house began to shake violently as thunder slammed down against the roof, completely shattering it. Rain then poured in from the ceiling, followed by raging wind, causing everything to fly out of place. Jean-Jacques wiped his eyes.

"Granme, where are you?" Jean-Jacques shouted as he found himself alone on the floor, drenched in rainwater. He ran to the kitchen and hid underneath the table.

The kitchen windows then shattered, and the back door blew open, lifting the table up and over Jean-Jacques's head. He quickly ran to the pantry and grabbed the doorknob, but the destructive wind swung his body around, raising him entirely off the ground. With all of his strength Jean-Jacques fought to close the pantry door. Water gradually poured in underneath the door, causing him to climb up to the top shelf. He then pulled the obsidian crystal from his pocket, closed his eyes, and prepared himself for a last breath of air.

To Be Continued.

## ABOUT THE AUTHOR

Warren O'Bryan-Adams is an American author based in Atlanta, Georgia. A native of the historic town of Tuskegee, Alabama, he has always had a special place in his heart for inspiring others to achieve their dreams through his fiction writing. Warren first began fostering his creative ambitions through blogging and sharing his short-stories with anyone who would listen before committing to a career as a writer. In his work, he explores various themes ranging from trauma, failure, spirituality, and self-identity.